Just the Thing!

With love to Rachel, Laura and Deanna –
the best back scratchers!
D.H.

For Matthew and Georgie
L.C.

Text Copyright © Damian Harvey 2005. Illustration Copyright © Lynne Chapman 2005.
First published in Great Britain in 2005 by Gullane Children's Books. Printed in Hong Kong.
This edition published in the United States in 2005 by Gingham Dog Press,
an imprint of School Specialty Children's Publishing,
a member of the School Specialty Family.
Library of Congress Cataloging-in-Publication Data is on file with the publisher.
Send all inquiries to:
School Specialty Children's Publishing
8720 Orion Place
Columbus, OH 43240-2111
ISBN 0-7696-4300-0
1 2 3 4 5 6 7 8 9 10 PIN 10 09 08 07 06 05

Just the Thing!

written by Damian Harvey
illustrated by Lynne Chapman

GINGHAM DOG
PRESS

Columbus, Ohio

Big Gorilla had a pesky itch
right in the middle of his back.
He wriggled and he squirmed.
He reached and he stretched.

But he could not scratch
the itch.

He hopped around the room,
scritching and scratching.
He bumped into walls
and knocked over furniture.
But he still could not scratch the itch.

"Shh," said Mama Gorilla, "you'll wake Little Gorilla with all this noise."

"You need a scratching tree. It's just the thing when I have an itch."

So, scritching and scratching, Big Gorilla went outside to lean against a tree.

He rubbed and he scraped. He scrunched and he scootched.

But the tree was all gummy,
and it stuck to his fur.
He still could not
scratch the itch.
And now his itch
was worse than before.

"It might be the thing
for Mama," said Big Gorilla,
"but it's definitely not for me."

"You should wallow in the mud," said Warthog. "It's just the thing for a hog with an itch."

So, scritching and scratching,
Big Gorilla stepped into the mud.
He wallowed and he wiggled.
He splished and he splooshed.

But the mud was too sloppy.
It splattered in his eyes and spluttered in his ears.
He still could not scratch the itch.
And now his itch was worse than before.

"It might be the thing for a hog," said Big Gorilla, "but it's definitely not for me."

"You should try
rolling in the grass,"
said Lion. "It's just
the thing for a lion
with an itch."

So, scritching and scratching,
Big Gorilla sprawled out on the grass.
He rolled and he tumbled.
He slid and he slithered.

But the grass was too slippery
and tickled his back.
He still could not scratch the itch.
And now his itch was worse than before.

"It might be the thing for a lion," said Big Gorilla, "but it's definitely not for me."

"You should try rubbing against an old anthill," said Elephant. "It's just the thing for an elephant with an itch."

So, scritching and scratching, Big Gorilla
leaned against an anthill.
He rubbed and he pressed.
He twisted and he pushed.

But the anthill was not old at all.
It was home to an army of ants!
They bit him and nipped him and
chased him around.
   He still could not scratch the itch.
And now his itch was worse than before.

"It might be the thing for an elephant," said Big Gorilla as he ran away, "but it's definitely not for me."

Big Gorilla raced down to the river and jumped in with a splash.

Then, scritching and scratching, he wearily walked back home.

He washed off the ants and the mud and the gum.

He was tired and wet
as he flopped on his bed.
And the itch?

It was worse than before!

"Let your dad rest," Mama Gorilla said to her son. But it was too late. Baby Gorilla had already jumped on his dad's back.

He wiggled and wriggled.
He scritched and he scratched.

"Mmmmmmmm," Big Gorilla groaned with relief. "Son, you're just the thing for a gorilla with an itch!"